We Read
PHONICS™

The Garden Crew

TREASURE BAY

Parent's Introduction

Welcome to **We Read Phonics**! This series is designed to help you assist your child in reading. Each book includes a story, as well as some simple word games to play with your child. The games focus on the phonics skills and sight words your child will use in reading the story.

Here are some recommendations for using this book with your child:

1 Word Play

There are word games both before and after the story. Make these games fun and playful. If your child becomes bored or frustrated, play a different game or take a break.

Many of the games require printed materials (for example, sight word cards). You can print free game materials from your computer by going online to **www.WeReadPhonics.com** and clicking on the Game Materials link for this title. However, game materials can also be easily made with paper and a marker—and making them with your child can be a great learning activity.

2 Read the Story

After some word play, read the story aloud to your child—or read the story together, by reading aloud at the same time or by taking turns. As you and your child read, move your finger under the words.

Next, have your child read the entire story to you while you follow along with your finger under the words. If there is some difficulty with a word, either help your child to sound it out or wait about five seconds and then say the word.

3 Discuss and Read Again

After reading the story, talk about it with your child. Ask questions like, "What happened in the story?" and "What was the best part?" It will be helpful for your child to read this story to you several times. Another great way for your child to practice is by reading the book to a younger sibling, a pet, or even a stuffed animal!

If we had a garden, what would you like to grow?

I'd like to grow a huge pumpkin!

LEVEL 6

Level 6 introduces words with "ey," "ie," and "y" with the long "e" sound (as in *key, chief,* and *sunny*), "oa," "oe," and "ow" with the long "o" sound (as in *boat, toe,* and *show*), and "ew" and "ue" with the long "u" sound (as in *crew* and *blue*). Also included are word endings -es, -ed, and -ly (as in *misses, started,* and *quickly*).

The Garden Crew

A We Read Phonics™ Book
Level 6

_____

Text Copyright © 2011 by Treasure Bay, Inc.
Illustrations Copyright © 2011 by Meredith Johnson

Reading Consultants: Bruce Johnson, M.Ed., and Dorothy Taguchi, Ph.D.

We Read Phonics™ is a trademark of Treasure Bay, Inc.

Published by
Treasure Bay, Inc.
P.O. Box 119
Novato, CA 94948 USA

Printed in Singapore

Library of Congress Catalog Card Number: 2011925875

E-Book ISBN: 978-1-60115-593-1
Hardcover ISBN: 978-1-60115-345-6
Paperback ISBN: 978-1-60115-346-3

We Read Phonics™
Patent Pending

Visit us online at:
www.TreasureBayBooks.com

PR-6-11

The Garden Crew

By Sindy McKay

Illustrated by Meredith Johnson

Picture Walk

Help prepare your child to read the story by previewing pictures and words.

1. Turn to page 4. Point to and say the name *Lizzie.* (You might want to say something like, "Oh, here is a name. *Lizzie.*) Then read the sentence to your child. "This is my buddy, Lizzie." Ask your child to point to the name *Lizzie,* and then point to the girl in the picture. Do the same with the word *Joe.*

2. On page 6, point to the words *Garden Crew* in the picture. Ask your child to look at these words on the sign and point to the same words in the text. Ask your child to read the words.

3. Turn to page 8. Read: *It had to be a sunny place.* Talk with your child about the kinds of things that plants, vegetables, and flowers need in order to grow.

4. Continue "walking" through the story, asking questions about the pictures or the words. Encourage your child to talk about the pictures and words you point out.

5. As you move through the story, you can also help your child read some of the new and more difficult words.

Sight Word Game

Memory

This is a fun way to practice recognizing some sight words used in the story.

Materials:

Option 1—Fast and Easy: To print free game materials from your computer, go online to www.WeReadPhonics.com, then go to this book title and click on the link to "View & Print: Game Materials."

Option 2—Make Your Own: You'll need 18 index cards and a marker. Write each word listed on the right on two cards. You will now have two sets of cards.

1 Using one set of cards, ask your child to repeat each word after you. Shuffle both decks of cards together, and arrange the cards face down in a grid pattern.

2 The first player turns over one card and says the word, then turns over a second card and says the word. If the cards match, the player takes those cards and continues to play. If they don't match, both cards are turned over, and it's the next player's turn.

3 Keep the cards. You can make more cards with other **We Read Phonics** books and combine the cards for even bigger games!

blue

yellow

pretty

soon

worked

our

very

they

some

3

Hi! My name is Joe. This is my buddy,
Lizzie. We want to show you our garden.

It was planted by all of the kids in our class.

The sign reads: Garden Planted by The Garden Crew

Our teacher helped us. She called us the Garden Crew.

We looked for the perfect place for our garden. We needed a place with lots of dirt.

It had to be a sunny place. Plants
need lots of sun to help them grow.

Next to our play yard was just the right place.

We drew a plan for the garden. We planned to plant five rows of seeds.

Then our teacher helped the Garden Crew sow the seeds. That means we put them in the dirt.

These seeds will grow into beans, peas, beets, and radishes.

We planted a few daisies too.

We planted them in *loam.* That is
dirt that has sand, silt, and clay in it.
Plants grow well in loam.

Our teacher gave us some ladybugs for the garden. She said they would eat the bad bugs.

Each day we checked on our garden.
We looked for weeds. We used a hoe to
dig out the weeds.

New seeds must stay wet. That part
was fun!

We did not let the seeds get stepped on. We worked very hard.

One day, the seeds started to grow.
The plants were tiny at first.

Then they grew and grew.

Soon there were lots of beans and
peas and beets and radishes.

The daisies started to grow too. Some of them were yellow. Some were pink. Some were white.

They were all pretty.

At last we harvested our crops.
Our teacher made a big salad for
us. It was yummy!

And the Garden Crew had
grown it all!

Phonics Game

Long "e" or Long "i"?

Creating words using new letter patterns will help your child review words in this story.

Materials:

Option 1—Fast and Easy: To print free game materials from your computer, go online to www.WeReadPhonics.com, then go to this book title and click on the link to "View & Print: Game Materials."

Option 2—Make Your Own: You'll need thick paper or cardboard, scissors, and a marker. Cut 2 x 2 inch squares from the paper or cardboard and print these letters and letter patterns on the cards: y, ie, a, b, c, d, e, f, g, h, k, l, m, n (two cards), o, p, r, s, t, u, v, and w.

1 Use the cards to see how many words you and your child can make that end with "y." Make words that end with "y" that make the long "i" sound, and words that end with "y" that make the long "e" sound. Examples with the long "i" sound: *by, my, cry, dry, fly, fry, shy, sky, spy, try, why;* examples with the long "e" sound: *penny, party, copy, any, many, funny, very, bunny, story.*

2 Then see how many words you and your child can make that use "ie." Make words with "ie" that make the long "i" sound, and words with "ie" that make the long "e" sound. Examples with the long "i" sound: *lie, pie, tie, die, cries, fries, flies, tries;* examples with the long "e" sound: *brief, chief, thief, field, yield, niece, piece.*

3 You may want to suggest a word for your child to make or even present the letters for a specific word. Or you can make a word yourself and help your child read the word. After a word has been made and your child reads the word out loud, see if he can change just one letter to make a new word.

26

Phonics Game

Musical Words

Taking a careful look at the words in the story will help your child to reread those words or patterns another time or in another story.

Materials:

Option 1—Fast and Easy: To print free game materials from your computer, go online to www.WeReadPhonics.com, then go to this book title and click on the link to "View & Print: Game Materials."

Option 2—Make Your Own: You'll need 12 index cards and markers or crayons. Write these words on the index cards:

Lizzie, buddy, show, crew, sunny, drew, rows, sow, grow, few, loam, hoe

1. Place the cards in a circle on the floor facing up and outward. Read the words out loud in random order while your child walks around the outside of the circle.

2. When you stop reading the words, your child stops and picks up the closest word.

3. Your child then reads the word out loud. If he reads it correctly, he keeps the card. If he reads it incorrectly, he puts back the card face down.

4. When all of the remaining cards are face down, turn the cards over and repeat. The goal is to correctly read as many cards as possible in round 1.

If you liked *The Garden Crew,*
here is another **We Read Phonics** book you are sure to enjoy!

Dad Does It All

Mom is sick in bed and asks Dad to do a few things around the house. Dad happily does it all: He cooks. He cleans. He even does the wash. Will Dad just make a big mess of it all, or will it all work out great?